AIRPLANES

Color & Story Album

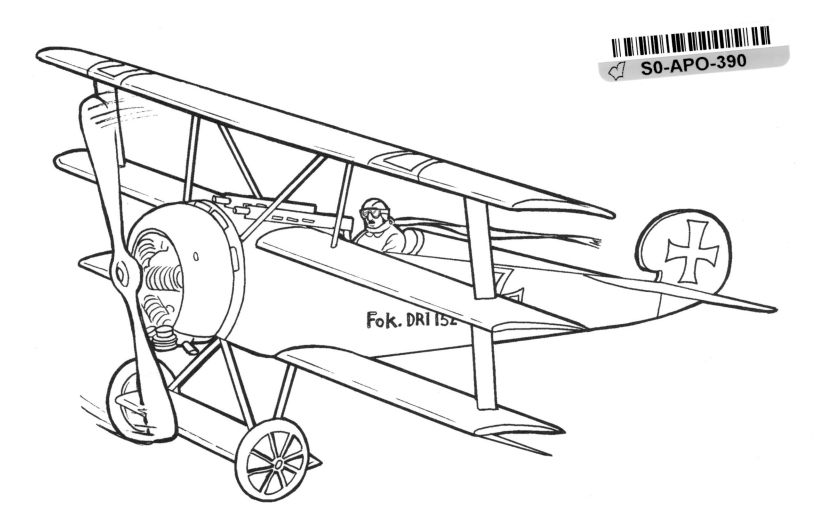

Written by Emily Neye
Illustrations by Renato C. Pia

TROUBADOR PRESS
an imprint of
PSS!
PRICE STERN SLOAN

ISBN: 0-8431-7855-8

1 3 5 7 9 10 8 6 4 2

Flyer

In 1903, Orville and Wilbur Wright put aside their work in a bicycle shop to build the legendary *Flyer*—the first-ever heavier-than-air flying machine. The *Flyer* was a simple marvel, with two propellers and two wooden wings covered with cotton cloth. It was powered by a small engine that ran on gasoline. Sitting in the middle of the lower wing, the pilot wore a wire "cradle" around his hips so that by twisting himself he could move the wing tips and maintain the balance and control of the plane.

Outside of Kitty Hawk, North Carolina, on December 17, 1903, Orville made history when he piloted the *Flyer* on its first flight. Their flying machine was airborne for 12 seconds, traveling 120 feet at 30 miles per hour. The Wright brothers were triumphant!

It would be a while before most people would learn that man had discovered how to fly. For two years, the Wrights continued with their experimenting and by 1905 they had built a fully maneuverable plane that could fly for half an hour. Finally, in 1908, Wilbur Wright made his first official public flight in France, amazing the world.

FLYER

Demoiselle

The Wright brothers weren't the only people experimenting with aviation at the turn of the century. Alberto Santos-Dumont, a Brazilian citizen who lived in France, also was a pioneer when it came to early aircraft. Like the Wrights, he spent years working with gliders and even tried his hand, quite successfully, at building dirigibles—those airships and blimps that look like giant balloons.

In 1906, Alberto became the third person ever to fly in a heavier-than-air machine. His plane looked and operated very much like a box kite. Later, Santos-Dumont went on to build a series of lightweight planes, including the 1909 *Demoiselle*. Made of bamboo and wood, the *Demoiselle* was easy to manage and to fly. It was one of the first airplanes that people flew just for fun.

DEMOISELLE

Sopwith Camel

World War I (1914-1918) was the first war during which airplanes were used in combat. The *Sopwith Camel* was a British biplane—it had two sets of wings rather than one—making it a sturdy fighter. It got the name *Camel* because it had machine guns mounted on top of a hump in front of the pilot.

During the war, airborne battles were nicknamed "dogfights" because the fighting planes had to do dangerous turns and rolls. Because it was so fast and well-armed, the *Sopwith Camel* was one tough dogfighter. However, it was not easy to control, so only the most daring, highly skilled pilots could fly it.

Today, the *Sopwith Camel* is famous for being the aircraft of choice for the cartoon beagle, Snoopy, in his never-ending dogfights against his arch rival, the Red Baron.

SOPWITH
CAMEL

Fokker Triplane

The infamous Red Baron, whose real name was Manfred von Richthofen, flew a *Fokker Triplane*—one of the swiftest German fighter planes of World War I. Built in 1918, the *Fokker Triplane* was known for its ability to ascend very quickly.

Richthofen was a sly fighter with shrewd hunting instincts who quickly rose among the ranks of the German Army Air Service. Eventually he commanded an elite corps of pilots. The Red Baron often flew a *Fokker* that was red. Because all of the pilots in his group flew brightly colored airplanes, they became known as "Richthofen's Flying Circus."

For each aircraft he destroyed, the Red Baron had a silver cup engraved with the combat details. By April of 1918, when Richthofen was fatally wounded in battle, he had quite a collection. With 80 victories under his belt, he was the top ace pilot of World War I.

FOKKER
TRIPLANE

Spirit of St. Louis

In 1927, Charles A. Lindbergh made the first solo, nonstop flight all the way across the Atlantic Ocean. Alone in his tiny cockpit, he flew 3,610 miles, from Garden City, New York to Paris, France.

Lindbergh was a modest and shy person, but also very brave. Many other famous pilots had attempted to cross the Atlantic, but none had ever made it. For his journey, Lindbergh flew the now legendary *Spirit of St. Louis*—a beautiful aircraft built just for him. *Spirit* was a monoplane, with one wing and a Wright engine. Because the trip was so long, *Spirit* had to carry large amounts of fuel. This fuel was stored in special tanks that took up most of the front of the plane. Unfortunately, they also blocked Lindbergh's view! In order to see where he was going, he had to look either out the side windows or through a periscope.

Lindbergh had fuel of his own: Loaded up with a thermos of coffee and a bag of sandwiches, he left New York on May 20, 1927. Thirty-three and a half hours later, he landed safely in Paris. He had made it! Greeted by a cheering crowd, the young pilot quickly became an international hero.

SPIRIT OF
ST. LOUIS

Curtiss P-40 Warhawk

The "P" in this plane's name stands for "pursuit." The *Curtiss P-40 Warhawk* was one of the United States' strongest fighters during the beginning of World War II (1939-1945). In fact, *P-40's* were used against the Japanese during the incident that brought the United States into the war—the surprise attack on Pearl Harbor in Hawaii.

Even before the U.S. became involved in the war, *P-40's* were well-known around the world. In China, there was a group of American volunteer pilots known as the "Flying Tigers." Their *P-40's* were painted like this one.

CURTISS P-40
WARHAWK

Military Air Transport Service

The *Military Air Transport Service* was an important part of the U.S. military in the 1940s. When the U.S. entered World War II, the *Military Air Transport Service* began to use planes like the one pictured here to deliver equipment, personnel, and letters from home to every part of the world where U.S. troops were posted.

During the war, the *Military Air Transport Service* had to expand very quickly. Everybody pitched in to help the U.S.—civil airlines supplied extra planes, and some civilians even became military pilots. The *Military Air Transport Service* was utilizing more than 3,000 transport airplanes by the time the war ended in 1945.

MILITARY AIR
TRANSPORT SERVICE

Canadair CL-215

The heroic *Canadair CL-215*—also known as the "Flying Boat"—is used to fight forest fires. Its lower half is shaped like the bottom of a boat, so it can take off and land on water or on the ground. While flying low over a lake or river, this plane scoops up water to fill its special holding tanks. It can carry more than 1,300 gallons. When the "Flying Boat" flies over a fire, the doors on the tanks open, and the water falls on the burning forest, putting out the flames from high in the sky!

CANADAIR
CL-215

B-52 Stratofortress

The *B-52 Stratofortress* was first introduced in the 1950s. Updated versions are still used today. *B-52's* saw a lot of action during both the Vietnam War and the Gulf War. They are particularly useful for ocean surveillance. Pilots of *B-52's* wear special night vision goggles that allow them to see the terrain below clearly even when it is dark outside.

Because these planes can refuel while still in the air, they can remain airborne for as long as the crew can hold out. During the Gulf War, a *B-52* made the longest strike mission ever when it flew from Barksdale Air Force Base in Louisiana all the way to the Middle East and back again. The mission lasted 35 hours straight.

LEARJET

AWACS

AWACS stands for Airborne Warning And Control System. These military planes have very fast computers on board and powerful rotating radar domes on top. The strong radar can pick up signals from enemy planes more than 200 miles away.

During a war, *AWACS* planes act as "flying command posts"—kind of like an airport's traffic-control center in the sky. Because normal fighter planes, military ships, and posts on land all have smaller radar ranges, they rely on the *AWACS* for important data.

AWACS

B-2 Stealth Bomber

The word "stealth" means the act of doing something secretly, and these hi-tech bombers truly live up to their name. Unlike regular planes, they can't be detected by radar, so they can fly into enemy territory "stealthily," without being noticed! Usually, radar works by sending out radio waves that bounce off aircraft and return to a detector. But *B-2 Stealth Bombers* are specially designed so that they absorb or scatter radio waves. So when radio waves are sent out, even if they hit a *B-2*, no signal returns. Nobody knows the *B-2* is there!

Unlike many other bombers, which require crews of four or five pilots, the *B-2* is operated by only two pilots: an aircraft commander and a mission commander. The U.S. government first unveiled the *B-2* in November of 1988, and it has since become one of their most effective combat forces. However, such advanced technology comes at a high price—each *B-2* costs about 1.3 billion dollars!

**B-2 STEALTH
BOMBER**

Concorde Supersonic

The *Concorde Supersonic* is the only airliner that flies at supersonic speed. "Supersonic speed" means faster than the speed at which sound waves travel, or faster than about 745 miles per hour. When a *Concorde* breaks the sound barrier, by flying over 745 miles per hour, it makes an incredibly loud sound, resembling an explosion, which is known as a "sonic boom." Because of this noise, *Concordes* are forbidden by law from flying over countries at supersonic speed. But even when they're not going more than 745 miles per hour, they still can travel faster than other passenger planes. Because the *Concorde* can outpace the difference between some time zones, you can leave Paris at 8:00 A.M. and arrive in New York City at 7:00 A.M. the same day!

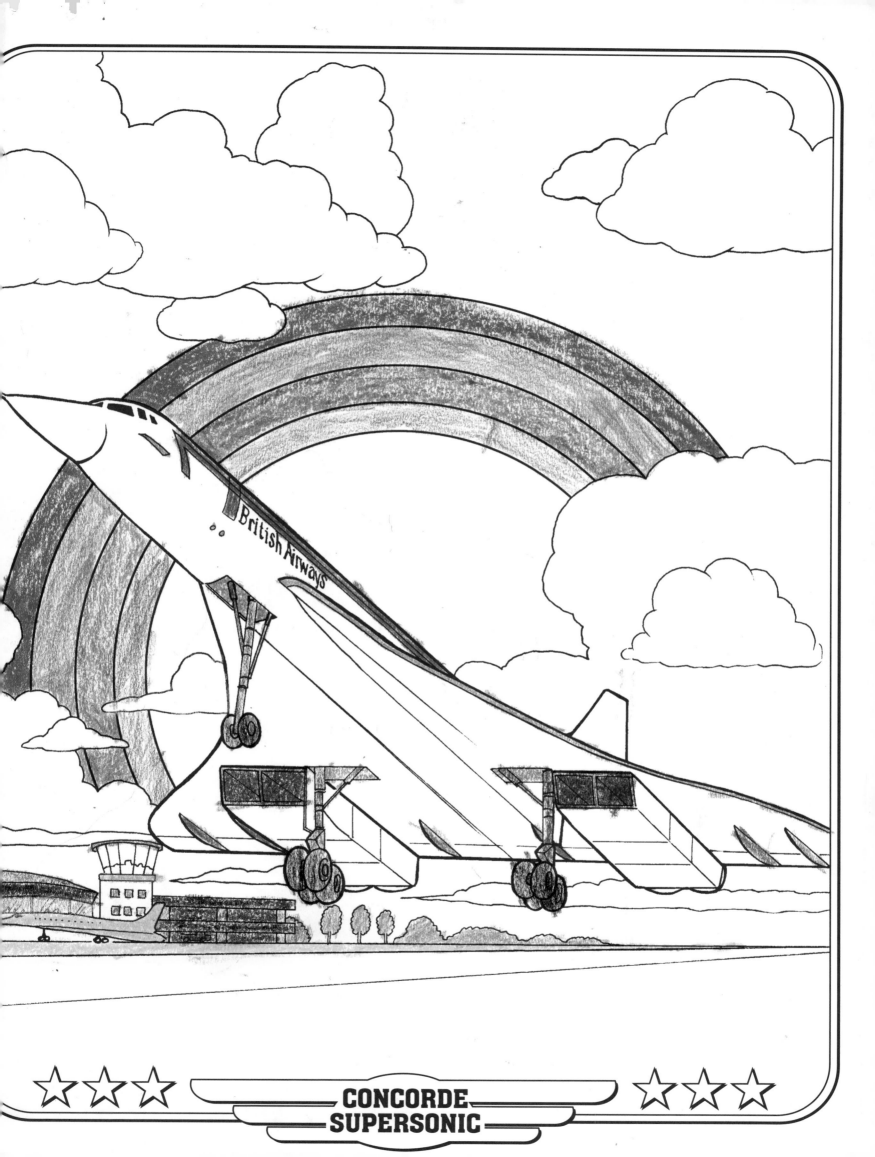

**CONCORDE
SUPERSONIC**

Air Force One

This famous aircraft was built to transport none other than the President of the United States. Special presidential air service has been used since 1944, in the days when Franklin D. Roosevelt was president. Roosevelt probably couldn't have imagined all of the modern features that are on *Air Force One* today.

Along with special electronic and communications equipment, *Air Force One* also includes extensive accommodations for the president and those traveling with him. The president's suite has a private dressing room, lavatory, and shower, as well as an office. There are also six other passenger lavatories and a conference/dining room. Of course, the president and his staff and guests may have to eat while they travel, so *Air Force One* has two kitchens capable of serving up to 100 meals at one sitting.

AIR FORCE
ONE

F-18 Hornets

F-18 Hornets are used for both defensive and offensive fighting. Often, groups of *Hornets* escort other fighter planes. They are famous for their reliability and durability. In fact, they are so easy to maintain that a *Hornet* can take a direct hit from a powerful missile, get repaired quickly, and be back in the air the next day.

The U.S. Navy's Blue Angels Flight Demonstration Squadron flies *Hornets* during their exciting choreographed air shows. The Blue Angels travel across the country, dazzling audiences with their dizzying aerial tricks.

☆☆☆

**F-18
HORNETS**

IMAGINATIVE
COLOR & STORY ALBUMS
FROM TROUBADOR PRESS

Airplanes   Exotic Animals

All About Horses   Giants & Goblins

Ballet   The Great Whales

Cats & Kittens   Mother Goose

Cowboys   North American Indians

Dinosaurs   Northwest Coast Indian

Dogs & Puppies   Trains

Dolls   Tropical Fish

Enchanted Kingdom   Unicorns

Wonderful World of Horses

Also look for our Troubador Funbooks and
Troubador Color-and-Find Hidden Pictures.

Troubador Press books are available wherever books are sold or can be ordered directly from the publisher.
Customer Service Department, 390 Murray Hill Parkway, East Rutherford, NJ 07073

TROUBADOR PRESS
an imprint of
PSS!
PRICE STERN SLOAN